Test
R.L.

Set 7

Level ~~4~~ 3.5
Points 0.5

The Ball⬤n Tree

Written and Illustrated by Phoebe Gilman

FIREFLY BOOKS

A FIREFLY BOOK

Published 1997 in the United States by:
Firefly Books (U.S.) Inc.
P.O. Box 1338
Ellicott Station
Buffalo, New York
14207

Original text and illustrations by Phoebe Gilman, copyright © 1984
Published by arrangement with North Winds Press.

Cataloguing in Publication Data
Gilman, Phoebe, 1940-
    The balloon tree

"A Firefly book".
ISBN 1-895565-82-0 (bound)   ISBN 1-55209-151-1 (pbk.)

PS8563.I54B34 1995   jC813'.54   C95-931193-9
PZ7.G55Ba 1995

5 4 3 2 1   Printed and bound in Hong Kong   7 8 9/9

For my three princesses,
Ingrid
Melissa
and
Alexis

Long, long ago and far away across a wide ocean there was a small, happy kingdom. In a big castle at the top of its highest hill lived the King and his daughter, Princess Leora.

Princess Leora loved playing and singing and dancing, but most of all she loved balloons. The castle was always full of them.

Then one day messengers came with an invitation for the King:

His Majesty, the
great King of Calloona,
invites your Majesty to a
royal tournament.
Please bring your bravest
knights.

"Can I come too?" Princess Leora asked.

"I'm sorry," said her father. "Not this time. But I won't be gone long, and your uncle will look after things here. I want you to help him."

"Not the Archduke!" Princess Leora said. "I don't like
him. He's grumpy and he never plays games. And what
will I do if something goes wrong?"

"Don't worry," said the King. "You can always signal me. Just gather a bunch of your balloons and release them from the tower. Wherever I am I will see them and come home right away." He kissed his daughter goodbye and rode off.

As soon as the King had gone the Archduke rushed in with the meanest guards in the kingdom. "At last! The chance I've been waiting for! Now *I* will be King. Guards, lock the Princess in her room and destroy all her horrible balloons. Destroy every balloon in the kingdom!"

Pop! Wham! Kablam! Princess Leora could hear the sound of balloons popping everywhere. How could she signal her father if she had no balloons?

But there was something the Archduke did
not know about — a secret passage that led
to the chamber of Leora's friend, the Wizard.
Quickly she slipped through a small opening
behind a curtain...

and entered a dark, twisting stairway inside the walls of the castle. At last she came to the Wizard's chamber.

"You must help me," whispered Princess Leora. Quickly she told the Wizard what the evil Archduke had done.

"There is only one thing to do," said the Wizard. "Find one whole balloon. Before the next sunrise, plant it under the tree that grows in the courtyard and say these magic words:

Moon balloon,
Moon balloon,
Tickle the tree.
Four balloons,
More balloons,
Blossom for me.''

The sun was setting as Princess Leora slipped through the castle gates to begin her search.

She visited the richest Lord in the city, but all his balloons had been broken.

She asked the butcher.

She asked the baker.

She asked the old toymaker. But no one had any balloons.

She looked through
dark alleys.

She hunted in the
empty marketplace
and knocked on
every door.

At last dawn was
near and there was
nowhere else to
look.

Sadly Princess Leora sat down by a small cottage.
The little boy who lived there heard her and came
to the window. "Princess Leora! What are you doing
out here in the dark?" he asked.

When the Princess told him why she had to
find a balloon before morning, a strange look
came over the boy's face.

"*I* can help you!" he said. He ran off inside
and came right back with a balloon. "When I
heard all the balloons popping I hid my last one
at the back of my closet. I wanted to keep it, but
you need it more than I do."

Princess Leora thanked the boy and ran back through the empty marketplace, past the stores of the butcher and the baker and the old toymaker, past the rich Lord's house and through the castle gates.

The moon was just beginning to fade when she came to the tree in the courtyard. She knelt down next to it, dug a hole and planted the balloon in it. Then she said the magic words:

"Moon balloon,
Moon balloon,
Tickle the tree.
Four balloons,
More balloons,
Blossom for me."

Suddenly the tree began to quiver. Tiny balloons blossomed on it and began to grow bigger and rounder. Princess Leora reached up to touch one and hundreds came floating down.

More and more balloons blossomed from the tree, until they filled the whole courtyard. As the sun rose they drifted through the gate.

People leaned from their windows and rushed into the streets, shouting and pointing and laughing.

"Pop those balloons!" the Archduke shouted to his men. But whenever they tried, the magical balloons whizzed away. Before long the whole city was filled with balloons.

All the shopkeepers had to close their doors.

All the chickens had to fly their coops.

All the traffic had to stop. Still the tree kept blossoming.

All the workers had to play.

All the schools had to close.

Balloons were everywhere. Still the tree kept blossoming.

The Archduke jumped up and down with rage when he saw that his guards couldn't pop the balloons. He rushed at the tree with his spear, but suddenly a balloon blossomed on its point, and he bounced right back on his bottom. Just then a balloon burst forth from the end of every spear. Madder than ever, the Archduke ran after Princess Leora shouting, "I'll get you for this!"

Far away, the King was riding through a dark forest when he saw a balloon caught on the branch of a tree. He thought that was a strange place for a balloon to be, but when he came to the edge of the forest he saw something even stranger . . .

His whole kingdom was filled with thousands and millions and *zillions* of balloons!

"Leora!" the King gasped. "She must be in great danger.
Back to the castle at once!"

When the King galloped into the courtyard he could see the Archduke screaming at the Princess. "You spoiled everything," he was shouting at her. "It isn't fair! *I* want to be King!"

"Princess Leora was right about you, you traitor," the King thundered. "Knights, put the Archduke and his men right where they belong — in the dungeon!"

Then the King invited everyone in the kingdom to the biggest party there had ever been. The people played and danced and sang. Princess Leora opened the royal treasure chest and gave everyone a present.

The balloon tree stopped blossoming as the moon rose,
but the party went on and on into the night. All the people
stayed up past their bedtime.

As for the Archduke and his men, they were in the
dungeon for a long, long time. But they were never bored.
They were kept very busy...

. . . blowing up balloons.